I would like to thank my father, Donald Bennett, for his photography of the KU campus and downtown Lawrence, with assistance from my mother, Margaret Bennett. A special thanks to Javier Lara Gonzales for author photos. Thank you also to Kay Yarnevich Smith and Collegiate Costumes for the use of the Baby Jayhawk costume on the cover. And a big thank you to Sunflower Outdoor and Bike Shop, Downtown Barber Shop and Sylas and Maddy's Homemade Ice Cream in downtown Lawrence.

-Jennifer Bennett

A portion of the profits from this book will be donated to Friends of the Theatre (FROTH), a support organization for the University of Kansas Theatre Department.

I am a Jayhawk

Requests for permission to make copies of any part of the work should
be submitted online at info@mascotbooks.com or mailed to Mascot
Books, 560 Herndon Parkway #120, Herndon, VA 20170

PRT0911A

Printed in the United States.

ISBN-13: 978-1-937406-08-0
ISBN-10: 1-937406-08-3

www.mascotbooks.com

I am a Jayhawk

I am a Jayhawk.

I walk the hawk walk.

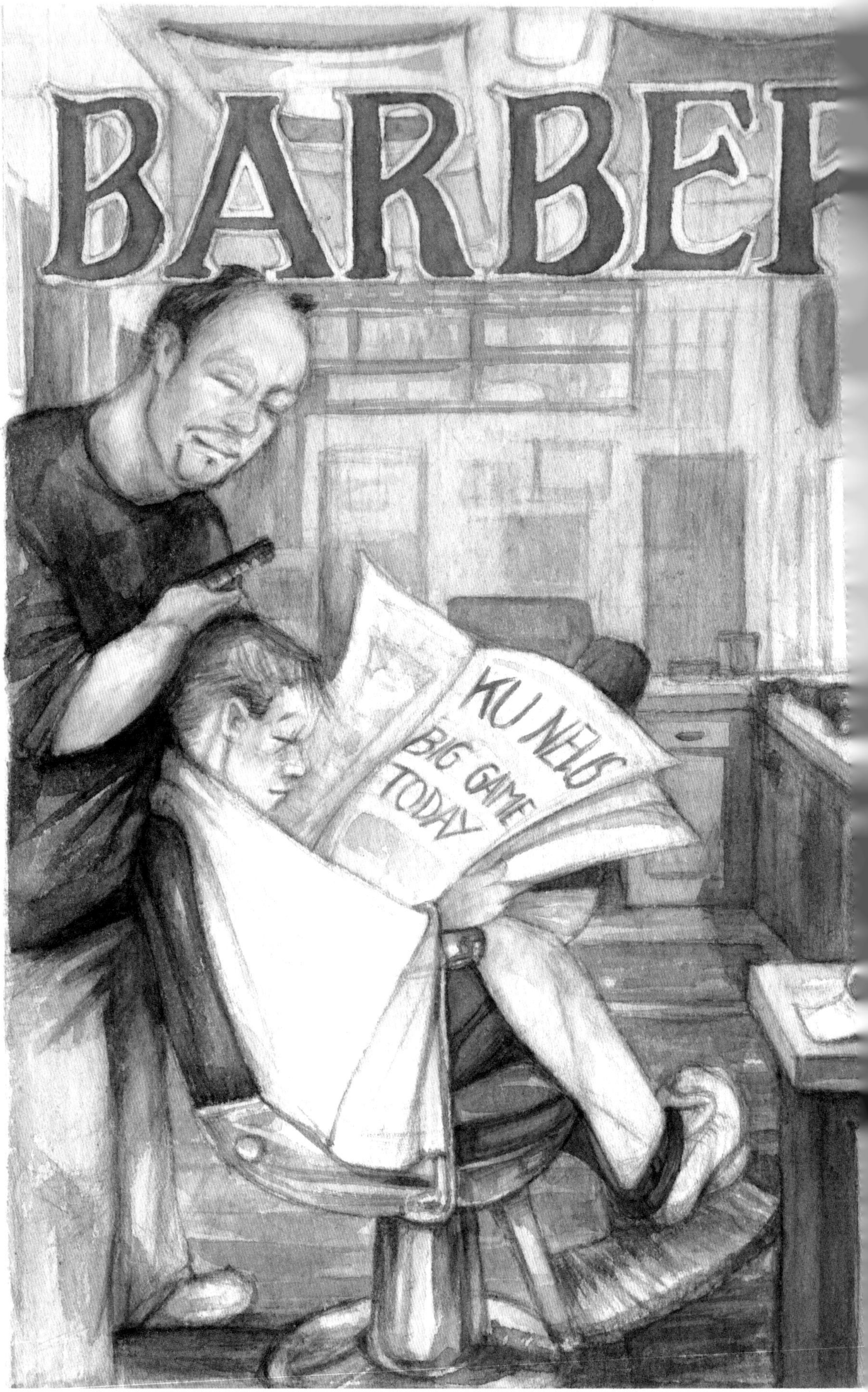
BARBE
KU NEWS
BIG GAME
TODAY

I talk the chalk talk.

I rock the
Rock Chalk.

I win the
big game.

Strawberry
Orange Sherbet
STRAW BERRY
Champions Choc
GOLD RUSH
blue moon
Grasshopper

I taste the
sweet fame.

Send 'em back...

from whence
they came.

'Cause I walk
the hawk walk.

I talk the chalk talk,

I rock the Rock Chalk.

I am a Jayhawk!

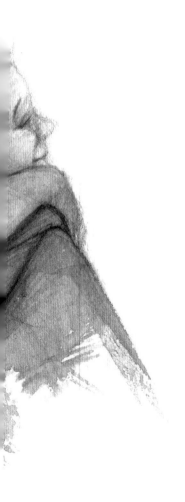

Rock Chalk...Jay-hawk...K

Rock Chalk Jayhawk KU! Rock Cha

Rock Chalk...Jay-hawk...K

Rock Chalk Jayhawk KU! Rock Cha

Rock Chalk...Jay-h

Rock Chalk Jayhawk KU

Rock Chalk...Jay-h

Rock Chalk...awk KU!

Rock Cl...Jay-h

Rock Chalk...

Rock Chal

Rock Chalk Ja...KU!

Rock Chall...y-ha

Rock Chalk Jaynawk KU! R

Rock Chalk...Jay-hawk

Rock Chalk...Jay-hawk

Rock Chalk Jayhawk KU! Rock

ock Chalk...Jay-hawk...KU

hawk KU! Rock Chalk Jayhawk KU!

ock Chalk...Jay-hawk...KU

hawk KU! Rock Chalk Jayhawk KU!

ock Chalk...Jay-hawk...KU

hawk KU! Rock Chalk Jayhawk KU!

alk...Jay-hawk...KU

Rock Chalk Jayhawk KU!

...Jay-hawk...KU

ck Chalk Jayhawk KU!

alk...Jay-hawk...KU

Rock Chalk Jayhawk KU!

k...Jay-hawk...KU

ock Chalk Jayhawk KU!

KU!

About the Author:

Jennifer Bennett lives in Granada, Spain with her husband Javier and their two children, Gabriela and Antón. Jennifer majored in English and theatre and film at KU and holds a Master's degree in theatre from Central Washington University. She teaches theatre at a bilingual Catholic school and writes original music for her folk band where she sings and plays the mountain dulcimer. She is the author of When You Were A Baby Jayhawk and co-author of A Tapestry of Tales. Jennifer, her husband, her two brothers and both her parents graduated from the University of Kansas.

1912

Illustrator: Ana Hernández Walta

I have been drawing and painting since I was a child, as the craft runs in the family. I can't remember a time in which the arts have not been my main interest. I graduated from the Facultad de Bellas Artes in Granada, Spain, earning an MFA in visual arts, and have been working on paintings, etchings and illustrations ever since.

To my family, for their endless support.

http://anahwalta.wordpress.com/